Happy Holidays

_____

PEARL'S EIGHT DAYS OF CHANUKAH

Pearl's Eight Days of Chanukah

STORY AND PICTURES BY

JANE BRESKIN ZALBEN

SIMON & SCHUSTER
BOOKS FOR YOUNG READERS

To everyone at S & S – a team effort, Anahid Hamparian, Michele Coppola,
and especially my editor Stephanie Owens Lurie.
To Helen Albertson, for her creative input, particularly the gold frame.
To Stefania Dispenza, for keeping me going.
To Uri Hurwitz, Hebrew scholar-in-residence.
To my family, Steven Zalben, Renaissance man, for his expertise, and
my grown sons, Alexander and Jonathan, although past the "activity" stage,
continue to give me infinite nachas in other "stages"—on and off,
and finally Zöe, who nips and licks my toes while I write and paint.

SIMON & SCHUSTER BOOKS FOR YOUNG READERS
An imprint of Simon & Schuster Children's Publishing Division
1230 Avenue of the Americas, New York, New York 10020
Copyright © 1998 by Jane Breskin Zalben
All rights reserved including the right of reproduction
in whole or in part in any form.
SIMON & SCHUSTER BOOKS FOR YOUNG READERS
is a trademark of Simon & Schuster.
Printed and bound in the United States of America
First Edition
10 9 8 7 6 5 4 3 2 1

Library of Congress Cataloging-in-Publication Data
Zalben, Jane Breskin.
Pearl's eight days of Chanukah / story and pictures by Jane Breskin Zalben.   p.   cm.
Summary: Eight stories and activities during Chanukah introduce the holiday and its
practices. Includes descriptions of related recipes, crafts, songs and games.
ISBN 0-689-81488-7 (hardcover : alk. paper)
1. Hanukkah—Juvenile literature. [1. Hanukkah. 2. Holidays.] I. Title.
BM695.H3Z35 1998
296.4'35—dc21   97-37917

Book design by Jane Breskin Zalben
The text for this book is set in Bembo.
The illustrations are rendered in gold leaf, colored pencils, and watercolor
with a triple-zero sable brush on Opaline Parchment.

Contents

Mama cried, "Pearl and Avi! Guess what, my lambs?"
"What?" they both asked, as they made paper chains.
"The twins are staying at our house for Chanukah."
"*The twins?*" said Avi. "All eight days?" Pearl asked.
Mama nodded. "Cousin Sophie will sleep in your room,"
she said to Pearl. "Cousin Harry will be in yours, Avi."
Pearl groaned. "What will we do with them for so long?"
Papa smiled. "Mama and I have plans. Big plans."
Pearl had overheard Grandpa call Harry a *vilde chaya*—
a wild animal. And Sophie was no little angel.
She once put a *latke* on Pearl's seat for Pearl to sit on.
As Pearl brushed her teeth on her last night alone
she wondered, would Sophie get to pick the colors
of the candles on the *menorah* because she was a guest?
Would Harry eat all the chocolate Chanukah *gelt*?
But most of all, would Mama and Papa have any time for her?

PEARL'S FIRST NIGHT

*A*unt Rachel and Uncle Solly brought Cousins Sophie
and Harry over the next day, just before nightfall.
They kissed and waved good-bye. "See you in a week."
The moment her parents left Sophie went limp,
like a *loksh*—a wet noodle.
Harry said he was already homesick.
As Mama polished her brass menorah, she had an idea.
"Why doesn't everybody make their own menorah?"
Together, Pearl and Avi got out Mama's big scrap box.
Pearl glued wooden spools and Avi used wooden beads.
Cousin Harry made his out of Sophie's curlers.
When Sophie realized that, she screamed, "I'm going
to flatten you like a latke. You're history, Harry!"
Mama wiped Sophie's tears and helped her bake a
menorah from homemade dough. While it was in the
oven, Papa used old plumbing parts for his menorah.
"Your Papa's menorah looks funny," Harry said with a giggle.
Later that evening, the menorahs lined the windowsill.
Pearl picked a bright blue candle for her *shammash*.
Sophie chose red. It was a good thing they each had their own.
They ate a nice hot meal, exchanged little gifts, and ran
around the dinner table as Mama and Papa gently tossed
them chocolate Chanukah gelt until they were dizzy.
Harry got most of it, of course. No one was surprised.

THE MENORAH

A menorah (also called a *chanukiah* or *hannukiah*) is a nine-armed candelabrum that can be made of wood, brass, silver, copper, pottery, even gold, glass or lucite. The eight arms represent the eight nights of the holiday. The ninth is for the shammash ("servant" in Hebrew), or helper candle that lights the others. The shammash, a slightly raised arm, is a bit taller than the other candles. At the end of each arm is a small cup to hold a candle or oil with a wick. Candles are placed in the menorah from right to left, the way Hebrew is read, but lit from left to right with the shammash so the newly added candle is the first one illuminated. Each night another candle is added to the menorah until, by the last night, all nine candles are burning brightly. It is customary to display the menorah in the window for all to see. Some families use an electric chanukiah with small light bulbs on top of each arm where the candles would be. Everyone in the family is supposed to be involved in lighting the menorah and enjoying its glow. A nice practice is for each member of the family to have their own menorah.

THE BLESSINGS

At sundown on the first night of Chanukah, these are the blessings that Pearl and her cousins said before the first candle was lit on the menorah. They smiled as the shammash and first candle burned brightly in the dark.

FIRST BLESSING

Blessed are You, Lord our God,
Ruler of the universe,
who has sanctified us by Your commandments,
and has ordered us to light the lights of Chanukah.

Baruch atah Adonai   בָּרוּךְ אַתָּה יהוה

Eloheinu melech ha-olam   אֱלֹהֵינוּ מֶלֶךְ הָעוֹלָם

asher kideshanu bemitzvotav   אֲשֶׁר קִדְּשָׁנוּ בְּמִצְוֹתָיו

yetzivanu Lehadlik ner shel Chanukah.   וְצִוָּנוּ לְהַדְלִיק נֵר שֶׁל חֲנֻכָּה:

SECOND BLESSING

Blessed are You, Lord our God,
Ruler of the universe,
who accomplished miracles for our ancestors
in ancient days, in our time.

Baruch atah Adonai   בָּרוּךְ אַתָּה יהוה

Eloheinu melech ha-olam   אֱלֹהֵינוּ מֶלֶךְ הָעוֹלָם

sheh-asah nissim la-avoteinu   שֶׁעָשָׂה נִסִּים לַאֲבוֹתֵינוּ

ba-yamim ha-heim baz'man hazeh.   בַּיָּמִים הָהֵם בַּזְּמַן הַזֶּה:

The *Shehecheyanu* is said the first time you do anything in the year.

(On the First Night Only)

THIRD BLESSING

Blessed are You, Lord our God,
Ruler of the universe,
who has given us life, kept us,
and helped us reach this day.

Baruch atah Adonai   בָּרוּךְ אַתָּה יהוה

Eloheinu melech ha-olam   אֱלֹהֵינוּ מֶלֶךְ הָעוֹלָם

Shehecheyanu, vekiyemanu   שֶׁעָשָׂה נִסִּים לַאֲבוֹתֵינוּ

vehigiyanu, laz'man hazeh.   בַּיָּמִים הָהֵם בַּזְּמַן הַזֶּה:

PEARL'S MENORAH

The cousins' menorahs were just for decoration, not for lighting.
Pearl's Mama and Papa helped with all the projects.

1. Pearl took eight small empty spools of thread and one large spool.
   Small spools are ⅞″ diameter x 1 ⅛″ height.
   Large spool is 1 ¼″ diameter x 1 ¾″ height.
2. In the garage, Papa found an oblong piece of wood about 1 ½″ x 10 ¾″.
   Pearl lined up the nine spools in a row. She put the shammash in the middle.
   It can also go at the right end.
3. She glued the spools ⅛″ apart, using wood glue.
4. Pearl liked the natural color of the wood, but Sophie thought she should paint
   the spools. (If you follow Sophie's suggestion, use a glossy paint or poster paints.)
   Papa and Pearl brushed one coat of varnish on the menorah.
   He opened the window to let the fumes out!

AVI'S MENORAH: Avi made the same kind as Pearl's, but instead of spools
he used ¾″ circular wooden beads that Mama got in a crafts supply store. The
beads were blue and white. He alternated colors. Avi put a white bead on top
of a blue one for the shammash. Then he followed steps two and three above.
Avi used self-hardening clay to make pretend candles to fit in the center hole
of each bead. He rolled different colors together to create swirls.

PEARL'S MENORAH

AVI'S MENORAH

SOPHIE'S MENORAH: Mama preheated the oven to 350 degrees. Then she helped Sophie make dough. In a bowl, they mixed: 1 cup flour, ½ cup salt, ½ cup room temperature water. They kneaded the ingredients into a ball of dough, then divided the ball in half. Sophie squirted 10 drops of blue food coloring into one ball, 10 drops of yellow into the other. They kneaded both again, and divided them into 5 blue and 5 yellow balls. Sophie flattened the bottoms, and lined the balls flush against each other on a cookie sheet, alternating the colors. Like Avi, she doubled one color on top of the other for the shammash. She rotated a Chanukah candle in the center of each ball to create a hole. Mama baked the menorah for 30 minutes, and allowed it to cool until it hardened. Papa added a coat of varnish. Sophie didn't miss her parents as much when she was busy. And Harry forgot about missing them too when he found Sophie's curlers! They were wide enough to hold Shabbat candles!

PEARL'S SECOND NIGHT

*P*earl spent most of the next day making greeting cards.
Sophie spilled glitter and gold stars all over the floor.
Harry and Avi played outside. Harry kept bopping him
with snowballs. Pearl stuck her head out the door.
"Hey, Harry, it's only the beginning of the week—
give him a break if you want to live to the end!"
Dusk approached as the pink sky turned to gray.
Before the first few stars appeared, Mama said,
"Bundle up. Tonight Rabbi Ramsky has invited the
entire congregation to hear the story of Chanukah."
"I can hardly wait." Harry rolled his eyes. Uh-oh, Pearl thought.
Everyone else was excited. They walked quickly to the
synagogue, smelling pine trees in the crisp winter air.
Sophie squeezed next to Pearl on the pew. Harry sniffed loudly.
"I smell latkes for the party. I hope they're as good as my mother's."
"S-sh. Quiet down," Pearl heard someone say behind her.
The rabbi lit the shammash and motioned for Sophie to
come forward and help him say the first blessing.
Pearl was envious. She had been practicing the blessing
for a whole week. Then the rabbi called Pearl to say the
second prayer. She felt better. When she was done it was so
quiet in the synagogue, you could have heard a *dreidel* spin.
Rabbi Ramsky began, "Chanukah is really the story of two miracles.
I will tell you about both." All the cousins huddled close and listened.

THE STORY OF CHANUKAH

"Once upon a time, King Antiochus IV of Syria ruled over Judea. He was a tyrant who wanted the Israelites to worship the Greek gods instead of their own one God. He put a statue of Zeus in the Temple in Jerusalem, commanded that sacrifices be made to idols, and changed the name of the city to Antioch. Some Jewish people obeyed the king's orders, either out of fear or because they liked the Greek way of life and no longer wanted to be different. Others became angry.

"A short distance from Jerusalem, in the little town of Modin, there lived an old Jewish priest named Mattathias. He and his five sons resisted the Syrian decrees. One of the sons was Judah Maccabee. In Hebrew, Maccabee means 'hammer.' Judah's determination, strength, and bravery inspired other Jews to join him in his rebellion against the king. When King Antiochus sent soldiers into the mountains after Judah and his men, they fought back. Although the Jews were fewer in number, they were fierce in their belief. Eventually they won, driving out Antiochus' army. The victory of the band of Maccabee warriors is the first miracle we commemorate during Chanukah."

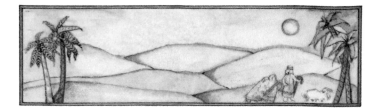

Pearl looked up at Papa, smiled, and sat on the edge of her seat, waiting to hear more.

The rabbi continued. "The second miracle occurred after the triumphant Maccabees returned to the Temple and found it ruined. After years of civil war, the holy books had been destroyed, and the holy oil, which was to keep the candelabrum burning at all times, was almost all gone. The Temple had to be cleansed and rebuilt. The statue of Zeus was removed. A new altar was erected. The priests brought in curtains and a candelabrum made of pure gold. There was only enough oil to keep the Temple candelabrum lit for one day, and it would take eight days for new olive oil to be made. Nonetheless, the little oil they had was put in the menorah so it could be lit for the Feast of Dedication. Chanukah means 'dedication.' The Maccabees rededicated the Temple in Jerusalem. Then a great miracle happened. The lamp burned for eight days instead of one. Judaism survived, as it has for over two thousand years."

The rabbi looked at the congregation. "The miracle tonight is, you're all so quiet, I either put you to sleep, or you liked the story."

Harry was about to clap, so Papa drew him close.

"You liked the story of Chanukah?" Papa asked.

"The best part was the fighting," Harry answered.

"I agree." Avi nudged Harry.

"I liked how Judah Maccabee was brave. We wouldn't be here today if it weren't for him, right?" Pearl asked. Papa nodded.

Sophie said, "Right!"

PEARL'S THIRD NIGHT

On the third day of Chanukah, Mama and Papa said,
"We're going to have a big, big party tonight."
Everybody spent the day—what else?—cooking.
Papa and Grandpa peeled and grated the potatoes.
Grandma fried the latkes. Mama made jelly doughnuts
from Uncle Solly's secret recipe, which he once
shared with Mama. Pearl, Avi, Sophie, and Harry
were measurers, mixers, and official tasters!
"*Ess, ess, mein kind.* Eat, eat, my child!" Grandma kept
pinching Harry's tummy. "Darling, you look so thin."
"Bubbe, please," Mama pleaded with Grandma as Harry
stuffed his cheeks. "There will be nothing left for the guests!"
Harry dipped the few remaining doughnuts into sugar.
Powdered sugar dusted everything and everyone.
It looked as if it was snowing inside the kitchen!
The moment Mama turned her head, Cousin Sophie
was up to her old tricks. Once again, she tried to slip
a latke onto Pearl's chair. Pearl caught her this time.
Sophie grinned sheepishly. She lent Pearl her favorite
ribbon for Pearl's party dress later that evening.
Friends arrived with food from their holiday celebrations.
Pearl and her family ate plum pudding and sweet potato pie
while everyone else had latkes, homemade applesauce, and
doughnuts oozing with jelly. "Triple yum," said Harry.

PEARL'S POTATO LATKES

Ashkenazi Jews, whose ancestors come from Eastern Europe, eat potato pancakes during Chanukah. Mama said, "The latkes fried in oil remind us of the miracle of the oil burning for eight nights." Mama, Papa, Grandma, and Grandpa helped by doing the hard parts—peeling, grating, and frying. Pearl, Avi, and her cousins did the easy parts—measuring, mixing, and tasting!

2 large eggs, beaten
5 large potatoes, peeled and grated
1 medium onion, peeled and grated

¼ cup matzoh meal
Salt and pepper to taste
Vegetable oil for frying

1. Grate peeled potatoes and onions by hand or in food processor.
   In a large bowl, combine beaten eggs, potatoes, and onion.
2. Blend in matzoh meal, salt, and pepper.
3. In a large frying pan, heat 1-inch layer of vegetable oil.
   Drop in 1 heaping tablespoon of mixture for each latke. A few latkes
   (about five) can cook at a time. Turn them over when crisp and golden.
4. Drain on double layer of paper towels or thick paper shopping bag.
5. Serve warm with sour cream or applesauce.
   (Pearl dips the latkes in chutney. Papa puts a pinch of cayenne pepper on his.
   Mama likes them just plain. She even eats them during Passover!)

Yield: 16-18 latkes, approximately 3″ round

AVI'S APPLESAUCE

8 large McIntosh apples, cored
½ cup maple syrup
2 cinnamon sticks (barks)

¼ cup raisins
1 lemon, quartered
Dark brown sugar to taste

1. Put whole apples in a large bowl. Pour maple syrup over apples.
2. Add cinnamon sticks, raisins, and lemon wedges to pot. Sprinkle brown sugar on top of apples. (Harry likes it sweet, so he added a bit extra when Avi wasn't looking! Grandma said, "What a *dreykup*." "What's that?" Avi asked. "Someone who stirs things up so much, you don't know whether you're coming or going! That's our little Harry!")
3. Partially cover pot. Simmer until the apples are mushy and runny.
4. Scoop out sauce from the apple skins, discarding skins, lemon wedges, and cinnamon stick barks. (Grandpa eats the skin. "You're throwing away the vitamins!" he protested.) Over a large bowl, mash applesauce through a fine-meshed strainer or sieve.

Yield: Serves 6–8 depending on the size of the dollops.

UNCLE SOLLY'S JELLY NUGGETS

Sephardic Jews are mostly descendants from Spain and Portugal, and some come from as far as India! A traditional Chanukah treat is jelly doughnuts called sufganiyot. *These treats, also fried in oil, are a reminder of the great miracle in the Temple. Uncle Solly shared his family recipe, handed down for generations, with Pearl's family. Mama and Papa did all of the cooking over the stove; the children helped make the small balls.*

1	package dry yeast	3 dashes salt	
¼	cup warm water	Dash of nutmeg	
1	egg, beaten	Dash of cinnamon	
1¾	cups milk	Rind of 1 lemon, finely grated	
½	cup (1 stick) butter	5½ cups unbleached flour, sifted	
¾	cup sugar	Large pot of oil for frying	

Grape, raspberry, or strawberry jelly, jam, or preserves
confectioner's sugar

1. In a small bowl, dissolve yeast in ¼ cup warm water for 10 minutes.
2. Add foamy yeast to beaten egg. Mix and set aside.
3. Scald milk in a small saucepan. Add butter to the hot milk. Continue to cook until butter is melted. Remove from heat.
4. When mixture is lukewarm, add sugar, salt, nutmeg, cinnamon, and lemon rind. (In the spice section of the market, bottled lemon rind is called "lemon zest." Use about 2 teaspoons.)
5. Add beaten egg and yeast mixture.
6. Put in large mixing bowl and blend in sifted flour. Knead until an elastic ball of dough forms. Cover with a dishtowel. Set aside in a warm area. Allow dough to double in size. Punch down after about 2 hours. Rip off pieces of dough to roll into small balls (nuggets) the size of walnuts.
7. Pierce center of each ball with skewer or knife. Put ¼ teaspoon jelly inside each ball. Smooth dough over with warm water to seal hole.
8. Heat enough oil for dough to float and expand in pot. When oil is bubbling, pop a few balls in at a time. Deep fry quickly (about 3 minutes), rolling ball around with a ladle until lightly browned. Drain on paper towels on a plate. Replace paper towels when they get greasy.
9. Put confectioner's sugar (about ½ cup at a time) in a paper lunch bag. Drop a few nuggets at a time into the bag and shake until dusted with sugar.

Yield: 3 dozen (if, unlike Harry, you don't eat any while you make them!)

PEARL'S FOURTH NIGHT

As usual, Mama had made too much food for the party
the night before. She lifted her arms in the air and said,
"What am I going to do with all these leftovers?"
Papa added, "There's so much food, there's enough
to last until Pearl's Bat Mitzvah!" Pearl had an idea.
"Let's take the food to the nursing home. I bet Rivka
and her friends would like it." Rivka used to live
next door. She had often baked for Pearl's family.
Now she was alone and Pearl thought, who was baking for her?
Mama and Papa smiled at Pearl's act of *tzedakah*, and her
thinking of someone less fortunate during the holiday.
Everyone piled into the car for the ride across town.
Rivka cried when she saw Pearl. Pearl wondered if she was
happy or sad. She sat next to Rivka during the song festival.
Pearl showed off her vibratos during "Rock of Ages."
Avi and Rivka clapped to "I Have a Little Dreidel." Harry
sang it ten times in a row until everyone covered their ears.
Sophie offered *rugelach* and Danish to Rivka and her friends.
Pearl smiled at Sophie, and Sophie smiled back.
Harry gave everyone a piece of the chocolate gelt that
he had been hoarding since the first night of Chanukah.

"Ma'oz Tzur"
(Rock of Ages)

—"Rock of Ages" is a popular Chanukah
song written in the thirteenth century, praising the many triumphs
of the Jewish people in history over religious persecution.

Andante (Majestically)

Traditional Hymn of Chanukah

Rock of a - ges let our song _____ Praise your sav - ing ___ pow - er;
Ma - oz tzur y' - shu - a - ti, l' - cha - na - eh l' - sha - bey ____ ach;

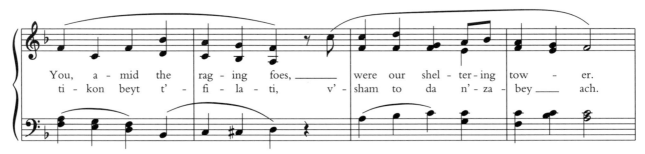

You, a - mid the rag - ing foes, _____ were our shel - ter - ing tow - er.
ti - kon beyt t' - fi - la - ti, v' - sham to da n' - za - bey ____ ach.

Fu - rious, they as - sailed us, But ___ Your ___ arm a - vailed ___ us,
l' - et ta - chin mat - bey - ach, mi ___ tzar ___ ha - m na - bey ___ ach,

And Your word ___ Broke their sword, _____ When our own strength failed ___ us.
Az eg' - mor b' - shir miz - mor, cha - nu - kat ha - miz - bey ____ ach.

Children of the Maccabees, Whether free or fettered
Wake the echoes of the songs, Where you may be scattered
Yours the message cheering, That the time is nearing,
 Which will see All men free,
Tyrants disappearing.

"I Have a Little Dreidel"

—This is a folk song for the game.

Folk Song Arranged by Jonathan Zalben
Based on S. E. Goldfarb

Allegretto (Gaily)

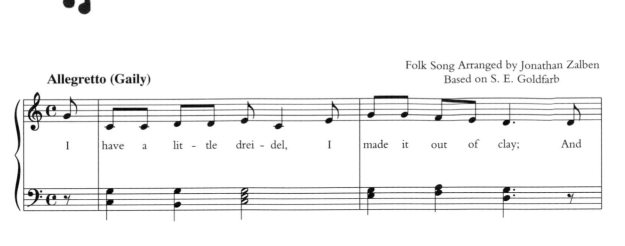

I have a lit-tle drei-del, I made it out of clay; And

when it's dry and read-y, then drei-del I will play. O drei-del drei-del drei-del, I

made it out of clay And when it's dry and read-y, now drei-del I will play.

It has a lovely body with leg so short and thin;
And when it is all tired, it drops and then I win.
O dreidel dreidel dreidel, with leg so short and thin
O dreidel dreidel dreidel, it drops and then I win.

My dreidel's always playful, it loves to dance and spin;
A happy game of dreidel come play now let's begin.
O dreidel dreidel dreidel, it loves to dance and spin
O dreidel dreidel dreidel, come play now let's begin.

PEARL'S FIFTH NIGHT

After so many busy nights, Mama and Papa welcomed
a quiet evening. They curled up in overstuffed
armchairs. The light of the menorah cast shadows
and filled the room with a honey-colored glow.
The children sprawled on their stomachs on the rug.
Then Sophie startled everyone. "Let's play dreidel!"
"And we could make them!" Pearl suggested.
"And spin them!" Avi shouted gleefully as he twirled.
"I'd better land on Gimmel, always. Or else I'm not
playing," Harry insisted. Pearl figured as much.
Cousin Harry was not a good loser. They spent so much
time spinning, they grew tired. One by one they fell
asleep on the floor, snoring gently, surrounded by piles
of chocolate Chanukah gelt, pennies, raisins, and nuts.

HISTORY OF THE DREIDEL

A dreidel is a four-sided top usually made of wood or plastic. It has also been made of lead, clay, brass, and even glass. Over 2,000 years ago in Judea, the Jewish people were forbidden by the Syrians to study the Torah, the first five books of the Bible. When soldiers passed by their homes, Jewish children would hide their books and spin dreidels. The soldiers would think that the children were playing with a toy instead of studying religion in secret.

In Hebrew, a dreidel is called a *sevivon* (spinning top). Each side is engraved with one of four Hebrew letters: Nun, Gimmel, Hey, and Shin (or Pey), which stand for the phrase *Nes Gadol Hayah Sham*: A Great Miracle Happened There. In Israel they substitute Po, which means "here," for Sham.

nun / nothing

gimmel. EVERYTHING

hey | get Half

shin \ put back one

HOW TO PLAY DREIDEL

Pearl's favorite Chanukah game is Spin the Dreidel. All four cousins sat in a circle on the floor with an equal number of nuts, raisins, pennies, or chocolate gelt (candy coins wrapped in gold foil) in front of them. Pearl explained how to play: "Each player places one thing from their pile into the center pot. Then we take turns spinning the dreidel until it stops. If the dreidel lands on Nun, you get nothing; if it lands on Gimmel, you get everything in the pot. If the dreidel stops on Hey, you get half of the pot, but if it stops on Shin, you have to put another object in the center. Whenever the pot becomes empty, we all have to put one object in before the next spin. The game is over when one of us has all the prizes. Then we can start over!"

Avi got nothing

Pearl got half

Sophie put one back

HARRY WON !

HOW TO MAKE

A DREIDEL

NOTES:

1. COPY THE DREIDEL DRAWING ON THE LEFT. DO NOT USE VERY THIN PAPER. ADD DECORATIONS OR COLOR.

2. CUT ALONG THE HEAVY DARK OUTLINE. ALSO CUT THE HEAVY LINE WHERE THE ANGLES INTERSECT. PUSH THE POINT OF A PENCIL THROUGH THE * ON THE TOP AND REMOVE.

3. TAPE A LARGE PAPER CLIP TO THE BACK SIDE OF EACH SQUARE THAT HAS A LETTER ON IT. THIS WILL MAKE THE DREIDEL SPIN BETTER.

4. FOLD ALONG THE THIN LINES. ALWAYS FOLD IN THE SAME DIRECTION, AWAY FROM THE DECORATED SIDE.

5. GLUE TABS MARKED 'G' TO THE BACK OF EACH MATCHING FACE. GLUE THE TRIANGLE FACES FIRST AND LET DRY. THEN GLUE TABS TO THE BACKS OF THE SQUARE FACES.

6. PUSH A PENCIL THROUGH THE * ON TOP AND THROUGH THE BOTTOM. IF THE PENCIL SLIPS IN THE HOLES, TAPE IT IN PLACE.

7. TWIST THE PENCIL BETWEEN THUMB AND FOREFINGER TO SPIN.

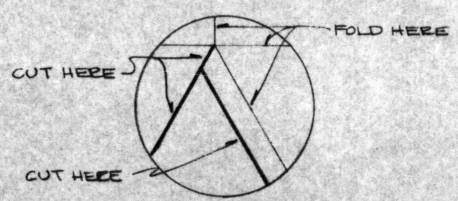

FOLD HERE

CUT HERE

CUT HERE

PEARL'S SIXTH NIGHT

*E*ach year Mama and Papa had a Chanukah hunt.
They would make and hide little gifts around the house,
leaving clues on tiny notes. This year, Pearl said,
"Let's make presents and hide them for the grown-ups to find!"
They made picture frames decorated with uncooked macaroni,
and sprayed them with gold paint. They carried many
boxes of old family photographs down from the attic.
"Here's a photo of Harry's first sleep-over at our house!"
Avi showed Harry the picture. "I look silly," Harry said.
He flipped the photo over, hiding his duck pajamas.
Pearl held up a photo. "That's us, when we were only
two years old, at Lake Cukamonga Bungalow Colony!"
"And our bathing suits match!" Sophie pointed out.
Mama overheard them from the other room and shouted,
"Grandpa sewed those suits out of leftover slipcover
fabric from Grandma's old couch!" She and Papa chuckled
as they listened to the cousins laughing and recalling
the numerous times they spent together as a family.
Once each cousin picked a photo to put inside a frame,
Harry taught everyone how to make wrapping paper to tuck
the gifts in. At last they were ready to begin the hunt.

Pearl left a note near Papa. "Br–r–r. What a draft."
Mama and Papa went to the front door. Everyone yelled,
"You're getting cold! Freezing!" As Mama walked closer
and closer to the kitchen, they yelled, "Warm, warmer!"
When Papa edged near the refrigerator, Pearl, Sophie,
Avi, and Harry jumped and shouted, "HOT! Boiling!"
Papa found another small note on top of the freezer.
"Z–z–z–z." One by one they followed Papa to the bedroom.
Finally, after six clues, Mama and Papa found the gifts.
"These are the best presents in the whole wide world!
We love them!" Mama turned to Papa and got all teary
when she saw the old photos of all the children.
"Where did the time go? They were so cute," she sighed.
"Hey!" they all protested. "We still are!"
Papa took Mama in his arms and hugged her tightly.
Everyone squooshed between them for a sandwich hug.

SPONGE PRINT WRAPPING PAPER

1. With a marker Pearl traced the outline of a six-pointed star onto an ordinary 3″ x 5″ kitchen sponge. Grandpa helped her cut it out with a pair of scissors.
2. Pearl dipped the sponge into a shallow tray of poster paint. She then printed stars onto glossy fingerpaint paper by pressing lightly with the sponge until the entire surface was covered. She had to wait until the paint was dry before she could wrap a present.

POTATO PRINT STAMPS

1. Avi asked Papa to cut a large potato in half. Then he drew a dreidel on the white surface of one half. Papa cut away the background around the dreidel to create a raised stamp.
2. Then Avi dipped the dreidel shape in paint and stamped it on brown wrapping paper.
3. Grandma helped Sophie carve a star into the other half of the potato. Then she and Avi shared their shapes and created a pattern.

PAWPRINTS

1. Harry did things the fast and easy way. He put his hands in fingerpaint, and then made handprints on newsprint paper. Grandma called it the *schmeer* technique. Luckily, Harry washed his hands afterward. Mama kept glancing at Harry's hands and her new kitchen wallpaper.

PEARL'S SEVENTH NIGHT

*P*earl was feeling sad. "I'm going to miss you, Sophie."
"Even though I hog all the blankets?" Sophie asked.
Pearl nodded. Mama noticed that Harry didn't look too
happy either. So Mama said, "Let's make invitations and
have a puppet show. We'll tell the story of Chanukah."
They picked names out of Grandpa's hat to decide
who would play each part. Pearl was Judah Maccabee.
Sophie was Mattathias. She laughed over being Pearl's father.
Harry got to be the evil King Antiochus.
"They're *both* tyrants." Sophie giggled.
"How dare you talk to the king that way?" Harry teased.
Then it was Avi's turn to pick. He looked confused.
Mama said, "You'll be the shammash puppet. I'll help."
Papa said, "And I'll help with the theater."
After they were done, the cousins delivered
invitations to a few neighbors. At showtime,
Harry nearly knocked the puppet theater over
during a major battle between the king and Judah,
but Avi saved the day by holding it together
since the candles weren't due on stage yet.
The show was a big success. They had three curtain calls!
"Next year, we'll do it even better!" Harry beamed.
Next year? Pearl thought. She hadn't had her parents to herself,
but in the end, she had to admit, they'd had a pretty good week.
"Sure, Harrala," Pearl said like Grandma. "Next year."
"I promise not to hog the blankets," Sophie added.
"I hog them too," Pearl admitted, giving Sophie a hug.

PUPPETS

Mama took out the scrap box that was filled with odds and ends for crafts.

1. For Judah and Mattathias, Pearl and Sophie made puppets out of wooden tongue depressors. They used yarn for hair and aluminum foil or cardboard spray-painted silver for shields and swords. Pipe cleaners were fastened to the back of the tongue depressor with tape for the arms and legs.

2. For King Antiochus, Harry stuffed one of Papa's old socks with Mama's torn stockings. He found three good buttons for the two eyes and a nose, which Mama helped him sew on the sock. He used yarn for hair, gluing it with craft glue. Then he painted a small gold crown for the head on construction paper, and found an old silk handkerchief, which he tied around the bottom of the sock head. This became a robe.

3. For the candles, Avi painted empty toilet paper rolls and glued glitter on the front. Then he pasted an ice-cream stick to the inside of each roll. He attached a thin piece of Velcro strip to each stick. Mama helped him cut a "flame" out of felt. He drew a face on each flame with a felt-tip pen. Avi pasted a tiny piece of Velcro strip to the back of each flame, so he could attach his flame to the candle. He crossed his thumbs in one roll for the shammash (which became a moveable shammash puppet), while the other rolls remained on the ledge of the puppet theater. That's how he had one big menorah!

Judah & Mattathias

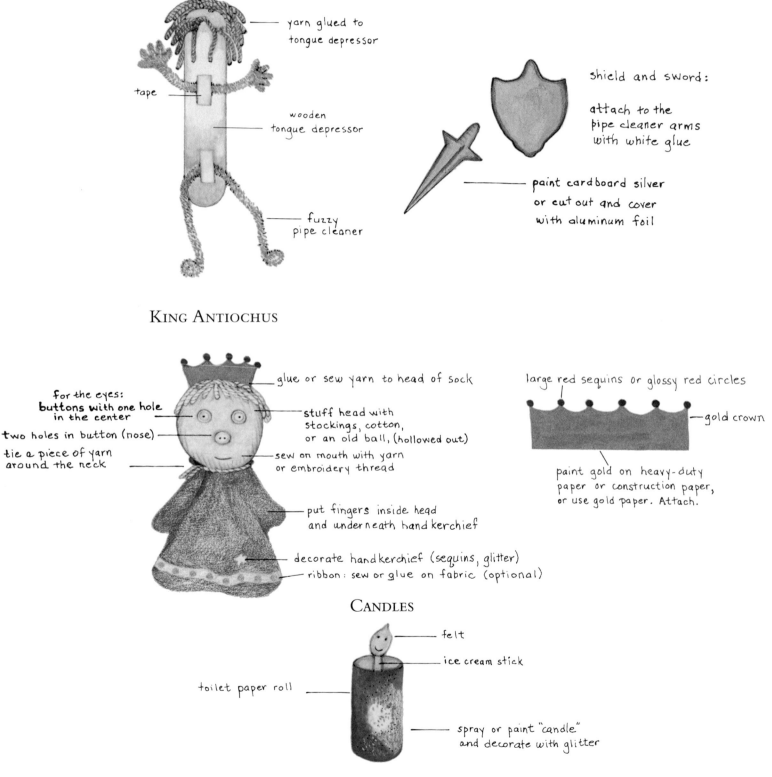

yarn glued to tongue depressor

tape

wooden tongue depressor

fuzzy pipe cleaner

shield and sword:

attach to the pipe cleaner arms with white glue

paint cardboard silver or cut out and cover with aluminum foil

King Antiochus

for the eyes: **buttons with one hole in the center**

two holes in button (nose)

tie a piece of yarn around the neck

glue or sew yarn to head of sock

stuff head with stockings, cotton, or an old ball, (hollowed out)

sew on mouth with yarn or embroidery thread

put fingers inside head and underneath handkerchief

decorate handkerchief (sequins, glitter)

ribbon: sew or glue on fabric (optional)

large red sequins or glossy red circles

gold crown

paint gold on heavy-duty paper or construction paper, or use gold paper. Attach.

Candles

felt

ice cream stick

toilet paper roll

spray or paint "candle" and decorate with glitter

PEARL'S EIGHTH NIGHT

*B*y the last night of Chanukah the cousins were
still talking to each other. "That's another miracle!"
Papa said with a smile. Sophie and Harry cried
when Aunt Rachel and Uncle Solly came to pick
them up to go home. "How were my sweet angels?"
Aunt Rachel asked. "Did they knock the *kishkas*
out of you?" Uncle Solly laughed out loud.
Papa looked down at Sophie and Harry.
"Sophie is now an expert latke maker
and Harry, a master latke eater!"
Harry announced, "We're coming back next year."
"But bring extra potatoes!" Pearl shouted.
Pearl watched them until they turned the corner.
The house seemed so quiet without her cousins.
Pearl thought, Maybe they will come for Passover in the spring.
For now, she decided to save her memories by
writing a story about her eight days of Chanukah.

MAMA'S MENORAH

by Pearl

This Chanukah was the best Chanukah I ever had. When
Mama first took the menorah down from the china closet
and unwrapped the smooth worn cloth, she said,
"My mama gave this menorah to me.
Someday this will be yours, Pearl."
Mama polished the menorah until the brass shined.
Her eyes twinkled as she held it up to the light.
"What is this spot?" I asked Mama about the chip.
"That happened when the menorah dropped off Great-
Grandpa Fishel's wagon as he was leaving Bialystok."
"And this writing, here?" I pointed to the bottom.
"Those are your Great-Grandma Gus's initials. She
celebrated Chanukah on the boat coming to America.
In the cabin below. She had the measles!"
Mama slowly traced over the deep scratches,
remembering her grandparents.
"And this tiny dent in the side?" I asked.
Mama laughed. "Your Aunt Rachel put a latke on my
chair when I wasn't looking. I sat on it, jumped up,
and the menorah fell onto Grandma's wooden floor.
Oy vey! Luckily, the candles weren't lit yet."
"I guess they were our age." I glanced at Sophie.

I put my menorah next to Mama's, pretending to light
the candle for the first night of Chanukah. I practiced
the prayers as I held the shammash over the candle.
Everyone lined up their menorahs along the windowsill.
During my eight days of Chanukah, we heard stories
and blessings, ate latkes and doughnuts, sang songs,
spun the dreidel, made menorahs and wrapping paper.
My cousins and I had a Chanukah hunt and a puppet show.
We visited an old friend who needed us. Earlier tonight
I carved today's date into my menorah with a pencil,
and whispered to my new doll as I hugged her,
"Someday, when you're grown up, this will be yours."
The candles were still burning in Mama's menorah.
They glowed brightly on the frosted windowpanes.
It seemed like a miracle that they had burned for so long.

GLOSSARY

Bubbe (BUH-bee): grandmother in Yiddish.

Bat Mitzvah (Baht MITS-va): ceremony for a girl who reaches the age of twelve, during which she is called to read the Torah, and becomes a part of the adult community.

Chanukah (CHA-noo-ka): (The "ch" in Hebrew and Yiddish is a gutteral sound, like in Bach or the Scottish word *loch*.) Chanukah (or some spell it Hanukkah) is the eight-day Festival of Lights celebrating the victory of the Maccabee warriors and the rededication of the Temple in Jerusalem. Chanukah means "dedication."

Dreidel (DRAY-del): four-sided top ("Sevivon" in Hebrew). The Hebrew letters Nun, Gimmel, Hey, and Shin appear on each side of the dreidel. They stand for the Hebrew words *Nes Gadol Hayah Sam*, "A great miracle happened there."

Gelt (GELT): like "felt" with a hard "g." Means "money." These chocolate coins wrapped in gold foil are given as little gifts during the holiday.

Kishkas (KISH-kehs): literally means "intestines." Insides, stuffings in Yiddish.

Latke (LOT-ka): potato pancake.

Maccabee (MAC-ka-bee): means "hammer" in Hebrew. Judah Maccabee and his band of brave warriors fought for freedom against the Syrians.

Menorah (Meh-NO-rah): nine-armed candelabrum lit and displayed face out in a window for each of the eight nights. Also called a "hanukkiah."

Rabbi (RAB-bye): the religious leader of a Jewish congregation.

Rugelach (RUG-a-lach): rolled pastry made with cinnamon, raisins, nuts, and raspberry jam.

Shammash (SHA-mas): "servant" in Hebrew, the "helper" candle that lights all the others on the menorah.

Sufganiyot (SOOF-gahn-nee-oht): fluffy jelly doughnuts eaten during the holiday by Sephardic Jews.

Synagogue (SIN-a-gog): a temple, a Jewish place of worship.

Torah (TOE-rah): the first five books of the Bible.

Tzedakah (Tzah-DA-kah): an act of giving to those less fortunate.